Refuge

OTHER BOOKS BY THE AUTHOR

Verse booklets

Learning Not To Touch (Redbeck Press, 1998)
Reaching for a Stranger (Shoestring Press, 1999)

Verse Collections

Outstripping Gravity (Redbeck Press, 2000)
Exposures (Redbeck Press, 2003)
Taking Cover (Redbeck Press, 2005)
No Time for Roses (Salzburg Press, 2009)

Narrative verse fantasy for younger readers

Wish* (Author-House, 2010)
(Due for republication by Thames River, autumn 2012)
Rainbow* (Due for publication By Thames River, autumn 2012)

*See also: author's website: www.michaeltolkien.com

REFUGE

-◆-

Michael Tolkien

 New Generation Publishing

ACKNOWLEDGEMENTS

The author would like to thank the recently-formed local Rutland Poets, a group with whom several problematic poems have been workshopped and 'rescued'.

Thanks are due also to Gordon Braddy, whose patient and perceptive reading and listening have guaranteed that many poems were profitably reworked.

For the last six years the personal and professional support of Darin Jewell (Inspira Group Literary Agency) has provided me with indispensable encouragement in face of many odds.

COVER ILLUSTRATION

Rutland Landscape by Rosemary Tolkien.

CONTENTS

I   *IN TOUCH*

II   *CLOISTER AND PROMENADE*

For Rosemary

...salted was my food and my repose
Salted and sobered, too, by the bird's voice
Speaking for all who lay under the stars,
Soldiers and poor, unable to rejoice.

Edward Thomas: from *The Owl* (1916)

I. IN TOUCH

NO GAME PLAN

Sweet Williams in a brown jug
you happened to find. Your dab of décor
for that sudden party, bright dice scattered
for a quick score. They wilt over
my unsorted mail, your rucked-up
half-read Tom Sharpe and a card
you once scribbled from breezy Margate.

Leaves curl to straw. Crimsons, maroons,
ivories fray like sun-worn curtains.
As I clutch and bin these stale virgins
in their washed-out gear and underwater
stench, I feel your gesture take its chance,
recall those whims that took a slap at time,
and turned my well-laid plans into a game.

IN TOUCH

When August tints and chills to autumn,
I notice how you cling to your clothes at nightfall,
complain that drafty spaces multiply in bed.

But look at the misty golden edge
round evenings closing in, vapours curling up
   in hollow places. Remember fire nights,
the primal hiss and crackle, how embers shift and wink.
   Be glad to batten down against a threat
that summons the snail in you, backing away and in
   to womb, cradle, a first room's embrace.

My fingers sift again through crumbled red earth
   after roots and spuds have done their work,
lie stacked and clamped. I sniff the final
   burning of a year's husks and straws,
walk from its passing blaze and smoke into
   your warmth, at ease with my autumnal need
to cover a space that makes me shiver.

ROOTED

Meandering funeral aftermath
finds us side by side
below the comforting splash
of tall, new-leaved limes.
Beliefs and sects creep
into our talk: how some suppose
no breeze can make them totter,
and most don't need to make a stand.
'So what are you now?' I ask.

'Nothing,' you say: assured,
precisely you, leaning a moment
on the chiselled hide of a lime
that knows where it stands,
as you do, gazing clear-eyed
past a blackened tower
to where you stood
and buried two parents,
not two springs apart.

THE YEARS IN 2006

Ibsen has been dead a hundred years.
   How many years ago
was Lise Fjeldstad filmed as Torvald's Nora?
   Lively, throttled wife who walked
out of their *Doll's House* and away
   from her stifling century.

In Oslo the hype blows over.
Loading a complimentary DVD
Lise sits down to watch herself
make history in Technicolor,
and finds she's glancing at a mirror.

Expecting to greet her face
with its familiar lines and cares
she confronts a lithe chameleon,
coaxing, devious, lovingly defiant
in her tormented rôle. Some youngster
moves, laughs and weeps like her,
yet makes her scowl in envy at a fraud
who sheds those intervening years.

TYPING OUTSIDE THE RAIN

On this cold, grey day, though tapping out
fretful messages on unceasing keys,
were you watching the deluge increase
over stone walls, scarcely breathing, anxious about
nothing much? As we who lack something of ourselves
can be.
Perhaps thick rain adds a shade more doubt.

Did this amorphous day that cloaked you cling
to your mind with wet lips and discontented breath?
Coffee, cigarettes, a few polite shows of teeth
and drenching walks were its gifts to your willing
body; yet you had to tread the only path
there was,
dimly curious about what premature night would bring.

Did one unguarded moment in this cold rain suggest
you might be too pliant
towards that seminar of bells and cant?
Perhaps as you filed another flat request
damp ends of hair brushed chilled fingers bent
on being
deft; and you paused at the edge of empty trust.

LOST

Safe as houses was her favourite tag
but at over ninety she was lost
in that steep-pitched, pebble-rendered semi,
floundering, too, since her husband died
trying to start his turquoise Cortina banger.
Slim, slick-haired, tight-suited, eighty-nine,
they called him *Tear-Arse Eddie*, terror
of the local roads. Police found
half a grand stitched inside his jacket.
High time to move her to a home,
her daughter told me, as if that was that.

Neighbours, who should mind their business
liked her pluck in carrying on regardless,
her backyard rites of broom and shovel,
the way she scraped and scrabbled for coal
from ramshackle bunker, poked up weeds and litter,
clattered out plates and cups for daughter,
who shouted in daily at four, and out at five.

In the small hours she'd come alive
and pace about with a swansong, racked
and cheerless as draughts moaning through a crack.

When rain dribbled down her bay window
she sat with opaque under-water stare,
watching her life trickle back. I'd wave,
and to wake her from that lonely deluge,
call in, brew a pot of strong, loose tea.
Yet her vacant eyes like blue-yoked eggs
gazed right through me and my chatter
at splashing traffic and bent, wet heads.

'Anything you need, Molly?' 'Larder's stuffed,'
her stock answer, waiting for me to leave
before she lurched off with giant strides,
jaw and stick thrust out, for odds and ends
or bargain Scotch for Eddie's safe return,

her silvered head with its skull-tight skin
so frail and intent, her frame that yawed
like a rudderless yacht, and left me helpless,
watching and praying from a distant shore.

UNSUNG

First met Bill delivering by van and bike
for a greengrocer. Needed to keep busy.
Newly retired from top management
in a firm tied up with North Sea Oil.
But why the collared neck? 'Cricked on the fairway,'
he said. Rumour was he'd mucked in
on the factory floor to dispatch a contract.

He'd nursed his wife into Alzheimer's,
resolved to keep her home at all costs.
When they caravanned in places coloured
with best memories, she'd wander off.
Police returned her wrapped in a blanket over
muddy pyjamas she'd fought to keep on
with snarls, bared teeth and clawing hands.

'Day Beth was taken in we'd been married
53 years. She scored 2 from a 30
aggregate of memory and response.'
Straight talk in a street encounter
while he looked beyond me as if to say
the broader picture must be seen, and added:
'Sense of humour's seen me through the worst.'

He's just over a heart valve transplant
and a ward infection that walled him in
for two months. Twice weekly he tees off
at 8 a.m. on the toughest local course.
And he's bought a compact caravan
to tour the coast of Scotland solo:
Stranraer, Durness, John O'Groats, Berwick.

I'm in open fields to lift the spirit
above self-created fret, and there he is,
striding out like a prospector,
his wilful little Scottie on a long leash.
Always one to seize the moment, this is
his bird day, delighting in rare flickers
of pairs and flocks in their spring passage.

VILLAGE BLACK SPOT

Double Z and nearly home, loaded
with seasonal gifts and looking forward.
Blind juggernaut like a crazed rhino
slews across and dumps its concrete pipes
on your one life in its egg-box shell.

What made you whole and loveable
cannot be prised from lacerated steel.
They couldn't even move you into
the sun like Owen's soldier with thoughts
of how its gentle touch once woke you.

Front page news between white on black
tributes to performance tires we need at speed,
your smile shy and modest above a catalogue
of family troubles that leave us at a loss.
Who were you? What lit up your days?

Then, full-spread, buckled, upended vehicles
as if some convoy had suffered a direct hit.
No hint of what is permanently shattered
and cannot be grassed over like bad bends
by-passed with three-lane dodgems.

NOTE: Wilfred Owen's poem *Futility* mourns a young soldier felled by a bullet but
apparently intact and unscathed:
'Move him into the sun-/Gently its touch awoke him once...'

HARDENED

Pine: young head
on bleached, spindly torso,
bending up from burned-out,
greening slope, your feet stood
firm and defied the flames.
Now you split my wide
sky and, like it or not, unzip
my acquisitive camera.

So what will you do beside
this washed-out track?
Mark a lurking hunter's path
that scurries into thorny scrub?
Let the odd passer-by pin
recurring hopes and fears
on your stooping trunk?

Look at me squinting up
at you, almost prayerfully,
my miniscule lens
capturing nothing much,
asking you to lose
no more plumage,
keep something back for
the next wave of lunatic fires.

FUSCHIAS

I fell for exotics like 'Mrs Popple'
who drapes her puce pagoda over
purple belly through which she hangs
her luminous fluted stamens.

Then I heard Norwegian Saeverud
paint her diverse tribe in piano notes.
His 'Drops of Christ-Blood' dripped
coral fire, aery pendants, fallen heads.

Now even Popple's plainer sisters
make me flirt. They're inverted,
shrunk crocuses, violently pink;
ruminating bells rung by
monologues of serious bees;
seamstress heads poised over
delicate stitches, at one
with their needles, at ease
with every cut-throat breeze.

Below their dancing show
springs a girth that thickens
into hedge. They bud relentlessly,
bear berries hard as ebony.

SACRILEGE AT THÉATRE DES CHAMPS ELYSÉES

Paris, Spring 1913

The Rite of Spring rouses berserk rival
ballet whose cultivated sneers, fistfuls of loathing,
Gadarene rush for exits, leave Stravinski
fuming over empty stalls. A thwarted god
ready to turn these deaf and blinkered
imbeciles to a herd of rooting swine.

Fine tuning and experimental sweat
have fashioned the clay's true guise
till nothing jars or niggles. Patterns
he wove to make the untuned hear
and taste the living earth, they tear
to shreds, piece by hated piece, shy
away from freaks and jackanapeses
writhing in mottled tights, birdsong
that scrapes like a rusty winch, cruel
thudding drum, jungle of fissured
string-play stampeding from the pit..

STASIS

Guitar held against long, white dress
you thread reluctant womanhood through
chords that waver in a question.

When time and tiredness beat you down
play back this moment. Listen for *Song*
that lives inside you.

Across your few furnishings and comforts
July sun throngs its last. Skylights brim
blue eyes wide. Your very breath's alert.

Fingers absently on strings whisper
over birdsong, flower, maze, water-
fall, ghosting in mind's own garden.

A zone of innocence swathes you,
holds this instant pressed in leaves
of sunlight, fading into attic beams.

Up here clock and weariness will
beat you down. Turn aside,
let *Woman* in you sing.

II. CLOISTER AND PROMENADE

MRS PRIMLEY'S LITERARY YOUNG MEN

(...Comfortable accommodation for male students in the Arts Faculty...)

Trunk and bags look lonely squeezed between
outsized bed and coffee-tinted wall
matched by threadbare floral counterpane,
starched and stiffened to withstand a fall.
Ladies in the bedroom not permitted!
insists Mrs P through pert and proper grin.
A nearly bald geranium in pitted
pot nods with dry dissent from sin.

O first-year hopefuls who unlock
cloudy-mirrored wardrobe doors, prize
open shallow mock-teak drawers, unpack
your dreams! Will this lumpy chair capsize
as you crouch to savour metered gas?
Can you feel the rug's biscuit patchwork
prick through thin socks after lonely traipse
back to pristine texts and dim-lit hack-work?

Don't miss High Tea at six
seasoned with Mrs P's prying talk:
egg on toast, shiny ham, lurid cakes.
Then how to bow out cheerily, stalk
away from deadlines on Damoclean strings,
and out towards hallowed lamp-lit recess
where Flavia the Fair in gown and kinky stockings
might come flowing from her bow-front fortress.

NOTE   Damocles praised Dionysius of Syracuse for his power and riches. During a
feast the tyrant suspended a sword from a thread over his guest's head to suggest the
instability of wealth and status and the imminence of disaster.

MR BUSY AND MRS: AN IDYLL

Mr Busy, oh so busy, up and down your drive,
past spruces well-spaced, tightly lopped and layered,
serene spires in glistening gravel...
off and back you drive, just for a little something...
(Busy are you, Mr Busy?
Lawn wants a trim, garage door's peeling,
leaves are going to clog the drain...)

Mr Busy's a mechanical man.
His paintbrush makes me dizzy.
So particular, so fussy:
Mr Busy's a busy mover.

' `morning Mr B_____! Nice day. Almost summery...'
    {{*Look! The morn in russet mantle clad...*
    How bloodily the sun begins to peer...}}

'Keeping busy then? Just the day for jobs.
Sorting the compost heap, I see. Plenty of tealeaves?
Off again now!'
(Smoothly does it in your shiny Roverette!)
    {{*... charioted by Bacchus and his pards...*}}

'Prescriptions. It's the wife, you see.'
'Oh dear! Well...if there's anything we can do...'

Mr Busy and his bungalow!
    {{*...one of the low on whom assurance sits*
    as a screw-top on a can of turpentine. }}

Busy bee keeping busy, making sure
the honeycomb's rich and snug
about his central-heated queen.

And there she is! Pink butterfly specs.
 (Nice and comfy, are you?)
Looks through conservatory triple glaze
on to shorn lawn, past Eight by Ten tool-shed,
over rolling fields ripe for sileage…and smiles.
'Mr Busy's mower's his life-support machine!'
 (Well that's funny, Mrs Busy.
Better check what Prudence brought
through the puss-flap.)

Mr Busy's snapdragons are well and truly visited by bees:
crimson, lemon, crimson, lemon, crimson, lem…

Everybody's busy these days,
minding their own business…

THAT YOU GEORGE?

Too much it was,
George,
what with rippled footprints,
crushed lilies,
buckled larger cans,
and those glittery fragments
catching dawn under the east window.

Then the shattered stone,
shale… slivers of shale,
George,
bits of *Beloveds, Sons, Nieces,*
tips of seraph wings,
vases full of shiny wrappers,
starlings raking through,
sparrows having a damn good chuckle.

As for the lytch gate,
George,
blooded all over with spray paint
and paving sledged apart…

Look on the bright side,
Eh George!
Friday night ringers at it again.
Hear that tun-up kid
taking a shortcut to hell,
thrush on his steeple tree
singing as if all were well.
And all that stone lying there,
like the stony dead:
think of that, George!

CLOISTER AND PROMENADE

Under sun canopy among
emptying tables, he reads and reads,
hunched over heavy A4 paperback,
cup, saucer and plate long forgotten.

Close-cropped, skeletal, hirsute,
all animation distilled into
his flickering, light-reactor
rimless spectacles. Enviably detached

from afternoon-long lunch party
in the teak-diner sanctum behind him,
aviary of jabbered opinions ignored
or gestured aside with ever-louder guffaws.

If he looked up would he notice
two little girls with no words in common,
sit side by side, strangership dissolved
in a shared pack of chip potatoes?

Or wonder if they might be sisters,
whose same brown, beady riveting eyes
and sticky fingers scour every inch and corner
where they happen to be this hot, sea-struck day?

Would he spot that silver-quiffed old gent left
by his burnished 50-something daughter
with a pick-me-up glass of white,
watch him cajole those heedless little darlings
with smiling, half-articulated warnings
that sound like final priestly blessings?

HALLOWED GROUND

If I speak with the tongues of men and of angels but have not love
I am become sounding brass, or a clanging cymbal (I Corinthians, 13, 1)

1. ON YOUR HIGH HORSE

Chapel's celebrating four hundred years
of scripture translated. Committee so much
wants you to take part. Well-known piece,
please, and any version you like.
Delighted ! How could you refuse?

Parted tongues of fire light your way
to Pentecost. ACTS, Chapter Two.
Might even fill them with Holy Spirit,
to find there's no foreign speech,
all words God's from time immemorial.

Must be the *King James* mustn't it?
Took unnumbered scholars eleven years,
rhetoric that rings with spoken sinew,
a voice for ever crying in the wilderness
to make straight the way of the Lord.

You'll stroll from pew to brass Eagle wings
where rests heavy tome sanctified
by years of blackening thumbs and fingers.
Find the place with reverence while noses blow
throats clear and shuffling feet fall still.

Airy shibboleths must give way
to what to wear and whether to tuck
that tight-packed quarto in coat pocket
or clutch and swing it to announce
the Lord's Day and where you're duly bound.

Unspectacular you scatter gravel
beside chequered, boldly-buttoned coats
and very practical handbags, filing in
by the narrow way, eye of the needle
into the fold of sheep the shepherd knows.

Not prepared for no-nonsense white-wash?
No hymnal, nothing to bow to, no pulpit
to declaim the Word interpreted.
A monitor displays the first hymn.
You'll sound like an over-piped organ.

All about you, sedate on creaking chairs
a genial crowd whose tucked-in postures
and hairdos bristle against airs and graces.
A modest book-rest on chrome pillar
awaits you with your fancy notions,
you with God's word and rows of patient faces
whose muscles would scarcely twitch if
Cretans and Arabians spoke in their own
day-to-day tongue the Lord's mighty works.
Be thankful for your words. Mouth them well.

One of the crowd at last you sing
a hymn with gusto till a shirt-sleeved preacher
preludes with glosses, then performs
from a Cockney New Testament
the miracle at the feast in Cana of Galilee.

OUR MAN IN THE OBERLAND

Kein weltlich Getümmel
hört man nicht in Himmel!... (Des Knaben Wunderhorn)

Soon to move on to another resort
he calls *Greendelvowelled*, he's solo
at a patio table picking at a punnit
of raspberries. "Hard to deal with
heavy meals here. So good
to sit with alpine panoramas. I get
strains from Mahler's 4th. You know the one
with that last song about *Heaven*?..."

We like his easy-care, sober dinner suit,
robust yet understated hiking kit,
his cool demand for consultation,
launching into schemes of 'heading out'
with such troubled doubt and rigour,
we're in the unknown and *he's* a pioneer.

Bleary-eyed at breakfast we're presented
with his 3D model relief map.
" Take it to plan your high-level trek
above that *tuna-whatsit* lake." (That's
the ice-blue expanse of *Thünersee*)
"Appreciated your filling me in
on ways down from that viewpoint
and how to take that quaint funicular
from the rail station by the river.
Noticed it's upgraded year by year!
So what do you guys do back home?"

Retired! We can't be serious! Active couple
like us must be mid-40s at most!

Farewell circumstantial buddy,
our own *Quiet American*!
There's no side to you. How come
you make us feel everything we say
opens up a whole new dimension?

NOTE Epigraph taken from the song mentioned in line 8:
you hear no worldly hubbub in heaven...

DINING

A threesome hogs sash windows that overlook
glabrous lawns, Friesans grazing their shadows,
distant cars glinting like trinkets in low sun.

   Club-Blazer-and-Tie breathes heavily over
his chins, seldom exceeds a phrase in rich, slow voice,
defers to his melon with a gentle forking,
lets wife and female crony make the pace.
   Queen Pin scintillates through blue-tinted specs,
emits chill fire at what she wants to see or hear.
Dressed down tight as disapproving lips
she wields a burnished hairdo set against dissent,
while flabby Number Three rumbles in agreement.

One tale ends with masticating nods, and
You'd think her parents would have had more sense,
then with melodious *quite right, quite right!*
perspiring Drop-Jaw fuels the next assault
with another round of Côte du Rhone.

Can the main course douse incessant talk
of who's who and others' mess and muddle?
Chewing adds relish to the moral. Every forkful
perfects the verbal stab and makes conviction
piquant till it hardens like the arteries.

Copper beeches blacken, mist creeps up,
haloes distant processions of lights,
while an agitating choice of suites is followed
by Remy-Martin, Grand Marnier, and Crème de Menthe.

Chatter shuffles to the hall, solid slams resound,
and gravel crunches under heavy wheels.

SPENT

White, uniforms converge bright-eyed
to coax, change and adjust him.
Young, eager to show no holds are barred,
they manipulate his bulk like navvies,
find purpose in sores, faeces, tubes,
maintain this flaccid mechanism,
once cock of the walk who reckoned to tread
every hen that fluttered across his path.

Now he sucks on each rationed cigarette
like a salving last request, wastes
his stock of words on what's served up
as food and who can't be *arsed* to visit,
swivels pale eyes up and down
these ayahs who rearrange his fragments.

EGO

You're *Alright Jack* passing moochers
who surely put on age like protective gear.

Wait till all those aches and niggles
entertained as passing blips, take root
                            and shoot
with mechanical precision.
Then try to get smartarse Jack
                        off your back.

Feel him tug when you hobble to
the coach after yet another toilet stop,
trying to spot your partner's hairdo.

If you're lucky and she's still there,
helping you trudge unlikely extra miles
on brittle bones and muscles drained of blood.

TOGETHER

Couples should fill us with hope,
walking with that assured clasp,
children again, wandering anywhere,
whimsical in their surprising leisure.

Such meanders, such pleasure in each other,
such florid dreams that cannot wilt or wither.

Forget those routine stairs their feet
will tread, rooms that seem replete
with cluttered memories and trinkets,
assumed like the bond of debt and habits.

IN THE CAFÉ OF YOUR CHOICE

She's half listening but I broach my fear
that options keep displacing one another.
"I'm doing X, and beyond return, knowing it
could have been Y, had I considered
as I now need to, α and β. Or even Z,
given the advantages I begin to suspect
of accounting for X,Y, α and β, not to
mention θ which has just occurred to me."

(Wait, though. The ageing gent over there
stares painfully at a cocksure trendy.
Why do I think he might object to fairisle
tanktops, slicked-down hair or a partner
having to listen to one or two notions
repeated in a hundred and one guises
over several capuccinos ?) "Perhaps," I resume,
"this shows my days are numbered and I'll lose
my appetite for taking algebraic stock."

"You'll get over it. It's tension,"
she says. "And too much isolation."
Now let me consider this very carefully,
I think I say, or am I mumbling ? "Next time,
and not just at one of these plastic tables,
I'll begin as I mean to go on:
setting out to find a solution."
Clearly though she's not impressed.

GOLD & SILVER

I.
♦

She censures our unruly world
with every step, and bourgeois gold
kindles her hair tossed here and there
to say *Try me! As if you'd dare!*

II.
♣

Marigold open to noon-day sun,
this is your now. You need not
be seed, shoot, bud or rot.
Unlike ours your cycle's just begun.

III.
♥

When her hair's thinned and silver
she'll look back and think proudly:
I found my own man and lover
and not a murmur disturbed me.

IV.
♠

Known mainly for tepid social grace,
she breaks out in sudden praise
for the lovely sound of silver and bell,
her tongue tingling with their spell.

POET BROADCASTS

1. *ME*

I'm all about myth re-explored.
You can't exhaust myths: everything itself
yet something else. Who needs empiricism!
I'll match A with B and see what arises:
lab.-work without a book of formulae.
I'm after anti-drama, coolly playing down
the awaited in a world that's *mezzo-forte,*
mezzo-relievo, mezzo-just-about-the-lot!

2. *IT*

Take this geranium stewing in its pot:
it brews aromas of damp nightfall
on the edge of woods over which a disappointing moon
hesitates in butterfly clouds that once
soared over the skies of your brittle childhood,
or maybe it was after you stepped from the car
in which Orpheus drove away from his terrible loss,
stung by the memory of a serpent in long grass
and of a swaying light, once a promising train
that resounded with half-forgotten melodies
before he'd lost his metro ticket…

Meeting a shadow of what she was
he'd noticed a slight twist to her mouth,
lobe-less ears, a high, glacial forehead,
how her left forefinger itched the air.
Was it worth encountering those monstrous guards
and officials with references and excuses in triplicate,
agreeing to ridiculous conditions for her release?

Even to this day he can't recall what she wore:
probably something pleated that bellied out
in the first blasts of upper air as he turned round
to warn her about snags in the cave floor…
And then the automatic doors closed
and he watched her looking for a seat,
shaking dust and damp wind out of her hair...

3. *CHAT AND CIAO*

A poem's like a boiling. Lid off too soon
or simmer too long, and it's fit for the bin.
A poet's Tweedledum self-communing under
an umbrella open for a theoretical shower.

Thanks for listening in…

NOTES PROVIDED FOR THE BROADCAST

1.)   One of many tales about the legendary Thracian king, Orpheus is how he
lost his young wife, Eurydice, to a snake who bit her as she ran from a man intent on
raping her. Orpheus, a spell-binding musician, descended to the Underworld, charmed
its fearful monsters and got permission from its king, Hades, to take his wife back to the
upper air, provided that he did not look back at her before they returned to the light.

2.)   In *Through the Looking Glass* when Alice asks Tweedledum if it's going to
rain, he opens an umbrella over him and his brother (Tweedledee) and declares it won't
be raining under their cover. Carroll suggests that their world is subjective, a matter of
playing with ideas. Tangible facts are of no concern.

DIVINITY THAT SHAPES

Commoditas quaevis sua fert incommoda secum.
Qunitillian

No wonder there was turmoil in Olympus
and the gods decided to nail Prometheus
for the theft of fire. By wielding fire
we flicker for a moment into gods.

Land, water, trade seem so much clutter
if history's a squabble for a share of fire.
Eating out our hearts for fire,
we've suffered the Titan's endless torture.

Now so few hoard such quantities of fire
the gods seem amateurs, and we who shivered
in caves cower from holocausts of fire,
naked to the bolts of nameless gods.

NOTE
Epigraph: *Every advantage has its drawbacks.*
Prometheus (of the giant race of *Titans*) was chained to a rock for ever. An eagle
devoured his liver each day after it had grown back overnight.

A LEVEL FANTASY

'...tell me, please, which way I ought to go from here...'
Alice in Wonderland

She'd been one to peck up every fact,
and he'd encouraged her in measured doses,
ticked margins and given way to *Good!*
Life-lines thrown out before she joined
the long roll of faceless names and numbers.

He'd fixed a grin to unwrap her gift:
Tenniel's *Cheshire Cat* framed and inscribed
It's been great! Nailing it up he feels
one grafter's respect for another.
She knew her *Alice* inside out.

Then after results a card of Alice
amazed by her golden crown, and thanks
that raised him to the angels. He replied
like some uncle puffing advice through pipe-smoke,
unseating every icon so she'd call it quits.

His reward was seven sides, close-written.
An essay he hadn't set… and so heartfelt.

TECHNODOC

O doctor, was there ever a time before
your trim cumulus curls massed daily
in menace over indigo-grey stripy tie
locked behind perennial hazy herringbone?

Countless formulae are noted, experiments
written up under your stony glint, distaste
honed on it, your barbed comments brushed off,
your nit-picking mimicked to a tee:

no buttons undone, no chewing, no yawns.
If you know what's best for you, don't gawp
or giggle, and learn to wipe that grin off your face.
Ginger, you're programmed with textbook cheek...

The only kids you'll father sneer behind your back,
plot to make boffin supreme blow a fuse,
while you engender gadgets and gismos,
checking dials and gauges with loving care.

All that laughter in eyes, brimming pools
truculently bright, eyes so ready
to sparkle, go cold in censure. Caught
in such precision sites, don't you cower?

Years clocking up hours and misdemeanours
with bitter smile over licensed after-duty moan,
a lemonade but *No crisps, thanks. Must go!*
Exit on cue to show we're lazy bums.

*

When you retire to fine-tune trouble-free engines,
sit behind *New Scientist* and net curtains,
won't the years' undercurrents ache back
like a lost pulse? They say you used to bend
iron bars like plastic cable. Hollow cheeks, doc !
Won't the years begin to bend you?

CARING PROFESSION

1. MENTORS

To you we're objects of fun or hate,
makers of pointless rules
who wield blades of sarcasm
at your defenceless ears,
fob you off with reasons
clean as forged notes.

You sense a hoax beneath the gloss,
an odour you can't define, and yet
your censure scatters like spread-shot.

Should we marvel at your deference?
It's the perfectly acceptable face
of the product we're paid to produce.

What eludes us is indifference
hardening like bone below the surface.

2. NUDGE FROM HESSE

Late October sun hallows heads
bent over books.

Don't be taken in.
This is not Castalia,
and you're not Joseph Knecht.

Nothing they read or write
touches their marrows
more than tomorrow's
foggy breath.

You dream of a *Glass Bead Game*
and this is just a gamble.
Odds on for grades or passes.

Come July, year in year out,
you'll pack away dice and cards
to clear the tables for another game.

NOTE In Hesse's futuristic novel, *The Glass Bead Game* (1943) Castalian society
disintegrates while an elite intelligentsia play an esoteric game in a quest for perfection.
When Knecht is appointed *Master of the Game* he tries and fails to redirect his
country's dwindling energies to practical questions and applications.

3. *RETREAT*

Late sleep. Shallow dreams
smother me in *Welcome Back!*
A gaunt-faced adolescent, one
in a hundred (boy or girl?)
agonises with dog-like faith
over the bones of an epic plot.

I shuffle through needs and queries
in files of scribbled notes (mine or theirs?)
stagger below them on familiar stairs.

But my bag of tricks is upside-down,
its jumbled conflicts strewn about,
churning round a river in spate.

I wade out, wrestle with the current
and wake up on the other bank.

No flattery will drag me back.
Let neglect howl over the waters
like famine. My flag is furled.

SOUNDS FROM A SHELL

White horsemen ride innocently
   over the green sea.
What if you try to disobey?
   Only men like you
   drown innocently.

White horsemen ride
   over the innocent green sea.
What if they decide
   to dismount?
Only such men drown innocently.

III. REFUGE

ENLIGHTENMENT

1. *FUSION*

Rage, rage against the dying of the light ... Dylan Thomas

Reading yet more print
into my bone-head to the near tick
of wooden clock
and dark roar of heavy jet
lumbering to defy gravity, lamplight

trembling in its filter, I burn
ever lower life's wick
vainly to ransack,
defying ignorance, others' worn
words from bone-heads that yearn

to bridge air's void with wooden
phrase or roar of ticking rhetoric
trumped up from trick
in brain's dark burden
burning to be said and heard in sudden

answer to clock and profane
roar of doom from pilot's stick,
defying fitful crack
of light rubbed up by bone on brain,
my dynamo dying as I strain

to read yet more print, defiant,
feeling heavy jet
smash the air, and set
my hand to trim the wick and hold my light.

2. GLIMPSES

Sometimes a lantern moves along the night
*That interests our eyes...*G.M. Hopkins

A light flickers
near or distant,
beckons towards a meaning:
someone taken away;
   a lone window swept
     by restless pines;
        drunks biking hell-for-leather
          down a rutted track.

No end to ruminations
on lights that flash persuasions,
threats, welcome; and then the stars
hoisting us up on chill, clear nights.

And, out of the blue, streetwise squibs
or inadvertent mirrors open cracks
that slap us where it hurts.

At full beam lights
bore in like blaring brass fanfare right
down the spine.

Nerve yourself along that frail
knife-edge path with a pale
torch that whimpers out..

But there are always lights
   near or far, refracting out the chance
     that distance
       won't fail...

3. *FESTIVAL*

Something white that glitters,
prismatically tinted,
littered with greetings, the odd
star, spire or holly leaf stuck
to its wadded mystique

A sentiment that rushes out
for the last one
six weeks before, then droops
penuriously gorged
when the avalanche stops
and goes grey.

4. BEYOND

They are all gone into a world of light... Henry Vaughan

It's not the closing down,
or fabled darkness and its worms,
insistent no-mores and last times
that make me ache and palpitate.

It's being the one to snap strings that tie,
and others left to pick up snagged threads
dangling in a heedless wind.

Now fading sight blurs what's beyond reach,
I savour at last the little within my clutch.

Yet new fissures
hint at worlds of light
nothing or no-one assures
me shine beyond sight.

OSLO TO BERGEN EXPRESS

Torrents recede to a faint hiss,
clinging birches mutter crisply,
a trapped gnat whinges in my beard
as I scramble up splintered rock
to a ballasted shelf hung
between rough-hewn cavern mouths.
Strung pylons crouch like alert reptiles
over sleek uncoiling tracks. Steely silence
defies breathing, makes the ears sing.

A beam's trace searches one tunnel wall,
bursts into a white eye blasting light
from aloof streamlined face that bears down,
screams by, antenna snapping blue flashes.
Skirl of steel biting steel curve, sucking draught
and sighing music of carriage after carriage,
rows of lights and heads, one surprised stare,
the last vehicle almost holding back before
the far portal swallows its red lamp.

Was this all I'd sweated here to see?
Or does watching an assured passage
that links lives with lives free me
from just letting another remote day
sink into dense tent-flapping night?

TAKING A CUT

New Year should mark a kind of survival.

It's just another day on this sodden pasture
creased with rounded strips. Stagnant pools
and mantled sludge fill the troughs between.

Ewes nose and fret among tarpaulined hay.
Spring will shoot wiry and tousled like the heifers-
in-calf and white-faced bullocks put out to browse.

Brothers hold the lease but seldom work in tandem.
On a bleak crown put to plough I watch Ivor
hitch shares and turn from three-furrow plod.

He's welded to his open-top, orange Nuffield
under torn cap and gaberdine so greased
they're wind-and-water-proof. Ready to chat

he notches back the throttle and scans ripples
he's sliced from this mat of bristling stubble. "Dry
underneath, just like powder. Look at it!

All that rain overnight! Where'd it go, eh?"
Scouring the ground with yardstick glance
he makes the cussed way of things worth a thought.

"Glad you're holding on to all your hedges," I say.
"We're stockmen. Beeves and ewes like a storm break."
I meet brown eyes used to sizing up beasts.

"Big farmer, Glooston way, ripped the lot out.
Gales scattered his top-soil after a March drought.
Harrow and drill again? Not likely. Too late!

Laid that hedge myself ten years back.
See how it's come on, except where my brother
made holes in it burning straw and stubble."

Chill January rain cuts us short.
He'll face it, grabbing up the iron crust,
firm behind wayward wheel and belching pipe,

though the yearly survival of stock is on his mind.

PROCESSIONAL

The year's moved house overnight
  and left a dismantled vault.
Trees are inscrutable, etched into
  basket-weave hedgerows.
A few sheep scattered over bald fields
  have stripped every green blade,
and latch on to roots. This high up
  birds of passage probe no loopholes
in a polar wind but dart from bush to bush.

  Northward one chalky cloud swells
like chimney-stack smoke against a zinc sky.

Icy gusts make up-hill work
  for a man and two youngsters
plodding across land knotted with sedge and tussocks.
  In shiny, warm, sensible clothes,
they might be nomads from any history:
  cloaked heroes claiming domains,
homeless fugitives in filched or borrowed dress.

  The children startle a lone crow,
watch it driven downwind; explore a hollow,
  pick up dead leaves. Their father
bends to listen and explain; but earth's parings,
  its stalk and bone, mean little.
They need to point and ask. He has to cast
  the spell of theory: rationale
of wire fence, pylon, cratered field, property.
  And they all hold hands
  to make reassuring headway
against the wind's senseless push and shove.

Sky's armoured grey is battered by gulls
  wheeling in cross-wind forays.

That one teeming cloud to the north has massed
  and flattened into drifting skeins.

AGES

Power lines whip round poles,
road and pavement run in spate,
hedges sag and swell, feeble as cress.

Business as usual, we trust,
yet we're primaevally old,
unfledged, shrink inside,
then into ourselves for shelter,
only to find fitful sparks
where a will once blazed.

Is our race about to lose
its feebly tightening hold ?

Look at those drenched kids
who dance and scream as if
to-day's deluge needs no tomorrow.

WAIFS

'What the devil can I do!' Hipcroft groaned
            (Thomas Hardy: **The Fiddler of the Reels**)

Festival of *Eighteen-Fifty-One.*
Enterprise and optimism glisten
in Hyde Park's glass cathedral, while London
sucks in the lost and undone.

Under Waterloo's iron awning,
jostled along a paved waste, mother
and child, unloaded from open, rattling
voyage like cattle, cling to each other.

Only a faceless surge of arrivals
and departures. Will *he* be there?

What with lean years corroding her
and this pinched offspring not his, he feels
their supplication too sodden to bear.

"How about something to stop the shivers?"

REFUGE

1. MUNICIPAL PARK

Triangular park railed between
converging lanes of heavy traffic.

Endless families alight on green
benches and parched grass, munch
picnics with far-away looks, wrangle
over ice cream or where to go next,
sidle off in loose gaggles,
while old mum and dad sit and sip
from thermos tops, doze, puzzle
over dried-up flower beds,
wait to be collected.

Crisp leaves rattle in circles,
a long summer's dust tangos
over gravel. Not so distant
cloud has whipped itself up
into a host of cobras.

Three women identically smart
dodge cars, vans, topless double-deckers
and take a break to show off the flimsy
contents of their logo bags.

Designer-clad covens and fully-padded
bikers glitter past, being seen together.

Sparrows have even more in common:
spasmodic chatter, pranks for ever
fizzling out to start again.

Then rain
hesitant and clumsy
after months of drought.

Which hardly matters to
some played-out busker
squatting on a playground log
or a frumpy pigeon that preens
and shuffles in a flattened sandpit.

2. IN THE GARDEN OF THE MUSÉE RODIN

A leaf spins down
and scrapes his shoulder.

Such soft percussion after
insistent crash of boulevards
wave upon wave…
then in Rodin's sanctuary
footfalls and angry sighs jostling,
nudging him on through modest rooms
stuffed with writhing sculptures, tight-lipped
daguerreotype families hung in brass,
carefully labelled stumps and blocks
that chronicle a clouding vision…

He who became a lunatic with no asylum
now stands still
on a path that tilts and dips
under balding trees, breathes his fill
of clammy decay, begins to feel
he'll measure up
to being mad again:

turned imbecile by hard facts and faces,
chased by volleys of wheels and lights
to take cover among falling leaves,
platinum ponds ruffled by smug ducks,
distant mothers behind prams, toddlers
in limbo, safely running circles…

Who can retrace such circles?

Will he always be heading straight
from A to B, or back,
only to check
his hell-bent intercity pace
in some unexpected garden
that hides from a wide confinement?

ALL

He had come to a meeting of roads we all
    reach, if we travel long enough.
Not like the fork that Robert Frost recalled: two
    paths diverging in a yellow wood.
Not a crossing of embroidered autumn lanes
    where the fingerpost made Edward Thomas
quell a mocking voice with stoical resolve.
    No: here you can't hazard a guess
like the young with all before them, take any turn
    because there's always another, swept towards
a mirage of endless chance, stacking the stakes
    high, spinning the roulette dizzy.

Here merge all routes he hoped to follow
    all at once, cheating the odds, tireless.
Like railroad junctions darting in beside a headlong
    train, all fold into one way ahead,
a beaten track more or less clear, its end known
    if not grasped, every choice he once made
    a looping round, often far round.

    Blind bends and dead ground
      promise no surprises now,
        only a hint of how
          an end will come, show
            up the whole quest
              for where it lead,
all doubts and queries put to rest.

IV. BELONGING

LOST AMONG PINES

[Basses Alpes]

Knuckled pine, miles of unbreaking waves,
spiked persistence, under it and underfoot
buried cones sprouting from quilted yellow needles.
Stand beside this ancient ribbed sea
that quenches its own thirst and try to
bear our frail girth and rootless passage.

Two well-hidden finches, shrill and upbeat,
making sure of each other across dry hectares
pierce the baked air. Are they near or far?
One day's niche in their dangerous trek,
a thousand miles of awkward looping flight
to seek out old haunts and new supplies.

They leave behind an arctic, green sighing
that sharpens the spirit as it wanders
on muffled footfalls, aware of loss, waste
what's owed to itself and never paid.
Will it stumble on some vista to measure
all this living, dying drought and juice?

Study muddled prints on a sandy track,
trying to trace some left by one loved beyond
bounds and time, her hand, voice and breath
too palpably absent. So why should solace
spring from one erect, sappy pine bud
pushing itself, like all of us, light-wards?

BETWEEN LIVES

'One is always nearer by not keeping still.'
Thom Gunn: **On the Move**

Moor without peak or fold,
untinged by low, steely sun,
sole way north a track
beaten into heather, then shivered
rock climbing to crumbled pillars,
entrance to rough-hewn bow bridge
pitched over gorge, its deep-delved
torrent a distant hissing ribbon.
Eyes fixed ahead, scramble
to its crown, and plunge down,
loose stonework hurtling away
to silent freefall. Pass broken arch
and feel upland turf underfoot.

Steep-raked birch woods simmer,
their olive-lit under-carpet
seethes with hue and cry of living.
Loose-clothed in shifting shadows
a rotund figure who might be
hunter, butcher, cook or wrestler,
cuts up a carcass, sculpting out
joints and chops with delicate art,
at one with his task and himself.

Nearby in sheltered, green dell
long, low thatched hut, walled
in wood and wattle. Its doorway
profiles a busy, slender woman
coarse-gowned, raven hair tied aside,
shimmering like breeze-blown foliage.

What account would they take
of some dusty, wandering drudge
who combs a wilderness for days,
chances a ruin to exchange
his nowhere for somewhere else?

FLIGHT

1.

A 747 oddly low for here.
   Caught in 8-mag monocular
      helpless floundering white belly
         puffs vapour scattered into crumbs,
            four engines pitched uncertainly
               between *head for land* or *soar*
                  and chance it in empty air.
                     Air-beached whale! Last
                  of its species about to
               go extinct on touch-down.
            Who can be aboard? Look for
         portholed heads filled with
      endless blue or capsized green,
   each looking for more than is there.

2.

In forest dusk two Muntjak bolt with crackling thuds
      over coppiced litter, turn stealthy,
         flashing white arse from
            trunk to trunk,
               pause,
            pick up caught breath
         and crepitating shoulder,
      slip along thread-needle pine trail
as the watcher cranes to sift hide from bark.

3.

In semi-darkness
stiff breeze shakes tatters.
Something amber dances in brambles.
Maybe a stray tag for rough shoot lot, rented
sliver of copse to stand all weathers and pick off
overfed fowl panicked by beaters into air, their last resort.
Fooled by a ragged balloon! Stretch its logo
and read *Malvern Scout Group*, just one
of jamboree helium-fuelled, bobbing
flights from a hundred miles
west of here, address tag
for kind return
still attached.

RESORT

I bus back to azure days of rock and sand
when dark seas pummelled walled bays,
children holidayed to bathe and dig,
feasted on sandwiches, hadn't learnt
to spend or felt the fear of missing out.

Alone up front on top I spot
a purple smudge beyond rising hills
that edge the sea in concave cliffs.
A black tor's wind turbine scythes
my landscape with maddening blades.

Tree-smacked the double-decker drops
into sheer-sided valley as if I drive
with abandon, lean into blind bends,
thread bottlenecks towards a stone town
that glints through thinning woods.

As we buck and brake at lights or road-works
I look up past fat-frying bars and gift shops
at faded Victorian hotels with their portals,
bay windows displaying well-spaced tables,
tall bedrooms behind nets and draped curtains.

I alight where strollers zig-zag up and down
shorn slopes that end in fenced-off crags
colonised by grunting, stiff-winged fulmar.
Far below a paddle steamer waits
to wallow out round long-deserted islands.

Not much footage unwinds from this patchwork
but here's a sandy inlet of barnacled rock
where we sat braced against wind and spray.
Reading *Bel Ami*, I laughed at something flagrant.
What's up, Daddy? (Don't Fathers know better?)

BELONGING

(*For Cathy*)

I.

  We're trimming stalks and husks
in a strip-light sunset, earth
sodden, moss-filmed, passive.
Your fifth autumn. You sift
my debris as if it's treasure,
neatly load the old barrow,
ask if mosquitoes dance
up and down spiders' webs.

  A question I needn't spoil thanks to
rooks lolloping west to roost
miles beyond our hedged horizon,
in twos or threes, some silent,
intent on return, some so gorged
with croaking chatter they slew off
course and swivel idly back.
And wouldn't you love to join them!

  If they were scissors, you say,
there'd be holes in the sky.

What's it like to be a rook?
"An ugly crow with pale face and beak.
Some might call you farmer's friend
but who'd want to live or work
near a woodful of yackers like you?"

  Easier said than what it might be like:
caught at dusk without a perch,
to drill at teeming fallow, mine for maggots,
shriek into dawn quarrel, taste
dry tongue as frost tightens.

  When *you've* flown elsewhere, I wonder,
will you notice knots of black wings
making for some distant comfort,
and think of homing rooks and home?

II.

Your age again, I'm all weathers
outside flint-rendered hotchpotch cottage
near woods of towering beech and ash
under rookery flight path, our bowed roof
streaked white from its restless traffic.

Look-outs cling to topmost twigs,
welcome back wandering droves
with all's-well bark. The sound
of permanence that makes it seem
we're planted deep in tree-lined shadows,

though I long for roar and swell
of thick-flocking autumnal spates
when cackling jackdaws and shrill crows
join the daily forage, return and squabble
over where to ride out the night.

*

Above us now tail-enders mutter
between wing beats, and I kneel
to help you scrape up our cuttings,

but I'm back among flattened bluebells,
knees black with leaf-mould, to rescue
fledglings flung from nests by gales
before their first, haphazard flight.

Never mind the blank stares and idiot squeals:
they're slop-fed in boxes by the coke boiler.
Tossed into aerial trials they flounder,
catch the knack, and never look back.

81

MOUNTAIN SUNDOWN

Low, lingering Norwegian sun
throws a birch pattern
over wood-clad room.
Most ponder their roaming day,
share it with postcards,
scribbling well-used phrases
that insist on being said,
miss the moment's fullness
when hard, clean light scrubs
crags and brittle crests of trees,
and its slow dwindling unveils
clefts, groins, fine-hatched crannies.

And beyond it all I'm seeing
one distant once-loved woman
sigh before her mirror,
expectant or listless about
an evening out, testing herself
against invasive light,
trying to shun the moment's weight.

AFTER THE SINGING

She lodged above a freezer shop.
He stood below her on the first dark step
beyond strip lights illuminating bargain buys.

Their concert so long rehearsed
with indifferent voices, was over.
Where should they go next?

Communal zest softened a broken past,
weekly shelter, somewhere to rub shoulders.
She shook and cried. He longed for her
to turn to him, sensing but not seeing
her morbid inwardness and taut temples.
He needed to cherish a crumpled face.

"I've been badly hurt. It ruins trust",
she said. "I'm the one who's always hurt,"
he said, feeling but not believing it.

Months later caught in the snare
of getting by and tired by devotion
that hadn't begun to heal her pain
she caught him unawares, hit him,
he felt, with what he'd said too easily,
before they stumbled up those dark stairs.

He traced the mean corners of her mouth,
flinched from a fretful soprano full of rancour,
and to hold his own, crassly declared:
"So...*Tempting fate* is more than just a cliché."
She consulted her watch, looked away
and said: "at least I've let you down gently."

THE ASSUMPTION

......*this*
both the yeares and the dayes deep midnight is.
(John Donne: Nocturnal on St Lucies Day)

I watch you
file drudgery away
on the night of the year's least light.
And I'm happy
for your respite.
Prospero's staff is broken. Aerial-free you flit
among cabinets, copiers, stationery.

Do I walk with you
in moon-clouded vault
of the year's midnight, or is it a trance?
Every thought
sways to a dance
as you waver in your tiredness and take a chance
with taunts and hints of affectionate sport.

O we've talked,
making every commonplace a comfort,
unquiet encounters this night will now eclipse.
Words cannot distort
heartfelt release
that says in no uncertain terms and not to please,
being loved from head to toe's your just desert.

But here's the lamp
where we are duty-bound to part
and night unlighted summons me away
to play another part
wearing hours away,
while you tread a straight, neatly-lighted way
with measured shadows that leave an undivided heart.

O the lamp inquires
and headlights probe as we stand
a pace apart in the year's longest night,
    and there's your hand
    limp and moon-white
like a question posed: welcome or withstand
this tender outbreak of long-restrained delight?

We're watchers
at the year's grave, benighted
under lamp-tinged brooms of ash that sweep beyond us,
    your face uplifted,
    traffic-lit, curious,
then snatched back, refusing to be sifted,
your breath charged and held, unutterably serious.

THE KISS

Recalling Vienna's Upper Belvedere
I recap from Michelin and smile
at how you'd prepared me for Klimt's *Kiss,*
dashing back up the hotel's four floors
for a postcard just to show me
how tenderly the man's hands rested.

Yet when we'd thawed out
from the Prince of Savoy's walks,
and stood before the original,
my eye ran down each pattern of a coverlet
that draped her, till I saw feet pointed
limply at her lover as if to match
her look of comfort and assent.
'Yes: we neglect our feet,' you said
in a voice that told me this was
your moment, and I wondered who
would rub yours to ease away their chill.

But the way those fingers touched without
taking, and the restraint of his bearded lips
made me turn aside with something about
reflexology and Chinese concubines.

LIVING SON

O zu ihr zuerst. Wie waren sie da
aussprechlich in Heilung...(Rilke: Das Marienleben)

No mirage shuddering in sunlit dust:
it was her son pale as unearthed root,
slow, strong pace so like his measured words,
wide gaze that stirred love and hate.
Fine-sculpted man broken and nailed
till he lost himself in a wild cry
and she left him embalmed and deftly bound.

The old rebuke came back: *His Father's business*
and didn't she realise? Yet light in foot and heart
she took his outstretched hand while his other eased
her shoulders of their tight-held grief. No words
for what had passed. So they begin again,
two trees that stir and sway to windless currents,
his work and hers now for ever one.

NOTE
Epigraph:
' O to her he first (came). Then and there how inexpressibly they were healed... '

PSALM

Forgive me, Lord, for not rejoicing
                  in her regard,
for waking to curse a wakefulness
that wracks me with distrust.

I have not asked for grace
to fulfil your promise,

I have not asked you to bless
the moments and makings
                  of our regard.
I have not freed my heart
to soar at your summons.

I have stopped my ears against
the songs she makes me sing.

                *

You have made me a place of rest to draw
                  on her regard.
    And I have not delighted
    in your loving kindness.

You have come brightening from the south
over a drenched land as we walked
                  in our regard.
    And I have not taken
    your sign to heart.

You have planted a seed and I have turned away
and left its tender shoots to wither
                  without regard.

A LIGHTER TOUCH

1. *ASCENT*

We tread higher into forest,
the path roughly terraced
by root and rock. Me first.

I turn and see you lit-up
in a glimmering gap,
your delight at each slow step

as if there's no other place
where earth's entire grace
could so enliven your face.

2. *EMBROIDERY*

I look out at midsummer borders
while tenderly a Purcell Almand's plucked
from harpsichord's fine-tuned wires,
elusive, fluid syncopations
that tint all you've nurtured and planted.

It's the rhythm of your fingers coaxing
into colour from green-winged fragments
wayward petunias, stocks, marigolds,
dahlias with pert looks and tuberous toes.

Is it you, Purcell, or the player
who brushes in layer by layer
this quavering melange,
pink-white, puce-yellow, mauve-orange?

3. *ILLUMINATION*

Does grubbing up weeds in August mist
purge me or do I fight some dogged force
that has to be admired and cursed?
What matter when your greeting
pitches gently into the damp air
and your smile, part question part blessing
strokes my face like a shaft of warm light?

It's the Feast of the Virgin's Assumption
and I face Mass to be beside you.
The sermon asks if we find Mary's joy
shining through the fogs of dogma,
for me no more or less your radiance
scouring a waste of potholes and minefields
I expect to fill and still for all eternity.

www.ingramcontent.com/pod-product-compliance
Lightning Source LLC
Chambersburg PA
CBHW051309250626
47155CB00009B/3493